Just One Goal!

Robert Munsch
Illustrated by Michael Martchenko

Just One Goal!

SCHOLASTIC CANADA LTD.

New York Toronto London Auckland Sydney
Mexico City New Delhi Hong Kong Buenos Aires

The illustrations in this book were painted in watercolour on Crescent illustration board.
The type is set in 22 point Minion.

Scholastic Canada Ltd.
604 King Street West, Toronto, Ontario M5V 1E1, Canada

Scholastic Inc.
557 Broadway, New York, NY 10012, USA

Scholastic Australia Pty Limited
PO Box 579, Gosford, NSW 2250, Australia

Scholastic New Zealand Limited
Private Bag 94407, Botany, Manukau 2163, New Zealand

Scholastic Children's Books
Euston House, 24 Eversholt Street, London NW1 1DB, UK

www.scholastic.ca

Library and Archives Canada Cataloguing in Publication
Munsch, Robert N., 1945-

Just one goal! / Robert Munsch ; illustrations by Michael Martchenko.
ISBN 978-0-545-99035-6

I. Martchenko, Michael   II. Title.
PS8576.U575J88 2008a   jC813'.54   C2008-903880-0

ISBN-10 0-545-99035-1

19 18 17 16 15   Printed in Malaysia   108   16 17 18 19 20

To Ciara Mapes,
Hay River, Northwest Territories
— R.M.

"A rink! A rink! A rink!" said Ciara to her father. "A rink on the river would be nice. I would not have to go all the way across town to play hockey."

"The ice on the river is a mess!" said her father. "It froze all jagged and bumpy. We can't make a rink."

"A rink! A rink! A rink!" said Ciara to her mother. "A rink on the river would be nice. I would not have to go all the way across town to play hockey."

"Too bumpy!" said her mother. "The river ice is too bumpy to make into a rink."

"A rink! A rink! A rink!" said Ciara to her sisters. "A rink on the river would be nice. I could walk right out the back door and down to the river and play on my own rink."

"Well, WE had to go across town to play hockey," said Ciara's sisters, "and that was good enough for us. So YOU have to go across town just like WE did."

"OK, OK, OK!" said Ciara.

She got a glass of warm water and a spoon, and went across the backyard, down the hill, to the frozen bumpy river. She used the water and the spoon to make a very small hockey rink — a good hockey rink for ants.

Ciara spent the whole next day carrying warm water down to the river. She worked till it was dark and the Northern Lights came out.

Finally her rink was big enough for a small dog.

Ciara's dad came looking for her and said, "Wow! A rink! You really made a rink."

"And I am just a little kid!" said Ciara.

The next day Ciara's dad rented a bulldozer and flattened a lot of river ice. Then all the neighbours came down and helped. By the time the Northern Lights came out, there was a real, people-sized rink on the river.

"A rink! A rink! A rink!" yelled Ciara. "A real rink on the river and now we do not have to go all the way across town to play hockey."

Ciara started skating and did not go to bed at all that night.

The next day, Ciara put up a sign that said "RIVER RATS RINK" and lots of kids came to play. But no matter what side Ciara was on, her team always lost.

One game that Ciara might have won ended when a moose went to sleep in the net.

Another game ended when a bear
chased everyone off the ice.

Another game ended when a bunch of teenagers raced through on their snowmobiles.

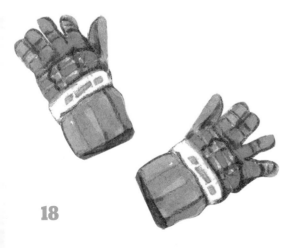

And that is why Ciara's team did not want to end a tied game just because the ice was a little wet. It was Ciara's last chance to win a game that year.

But suddenly, the rink started floating down the river while the rest of the ice crashed and boomed around it.

The players did not even notice.

Ciara's mom noticed.

"AHHHHHHHHHHH!" yelled Ciara's mom. "BREAKUP!"

She ran along the river yelling "STOP! STOP! STOP!" but the players could not hear because the ice was making so much noise.

Ciara's father ran along the river yelling "STOP! STOP! STOP!" but the players could not hear because the ice was making so much noise.

Then all the parents ran along the river yelling "STOP! STOP! STOP!" but the teams just kept playing.

"The bridge!" yelled Ciara's mom. "We can catch them at the bridge!"

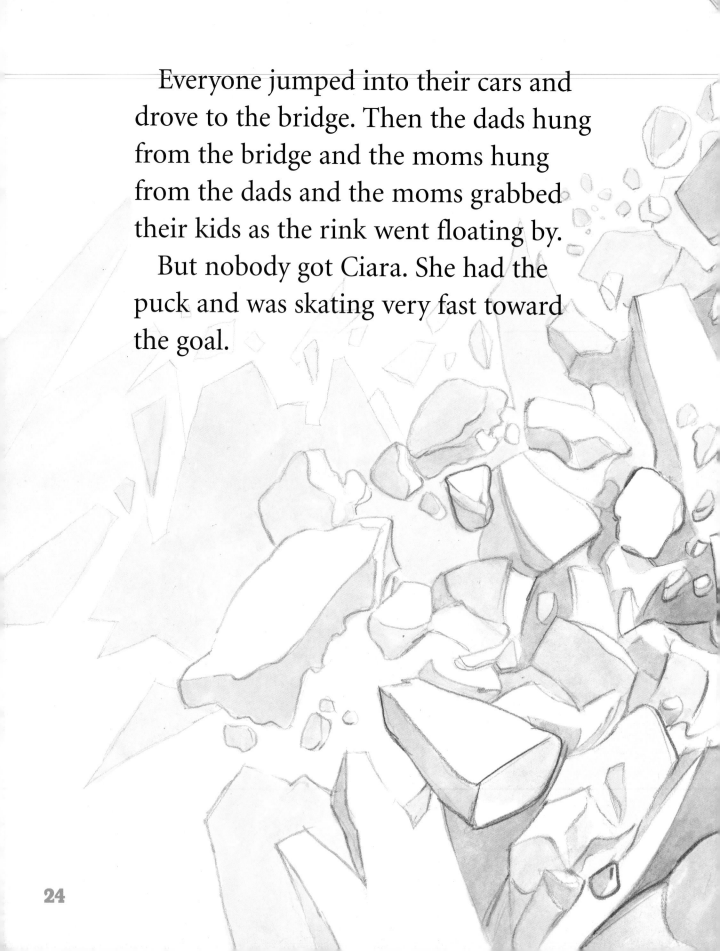

Everyone jumped into their cars and drove to the bridge. Then the dads hung from the bridge and the moms hung from the dads and the moms grabbed their kids as the rink went floating by.

But nobody got Ciara. She had the puck and was skating very fast toward the goal.

Ciara's dad ran to his car, got his fishing rod, and cast his hook way, way, way down the river.